W9-DIW-200

OYOTE FIGHTS THE SUN

CXRR
P2
7
.C37646
Co
2002

OYOTE FIGHTS

THE SUN

Shasta Indian Tale

Mary J. Carpelan

Heyday Books • Berkeley, California

Library of Congress Cataloging-in-Publication Data

Carpelan, Mary J., 1953-
    Coyote fights the sun : a Shasta Indian tale / Mary J. Carpelan.
      p. cm.
    Summary: A retelling of the traditional Shasta Indian tale in
  which Coyote decides to shoot the sun for misleading him about
  the coming of spring.
    ISBN 1-890771-60-0 (alk. paper)
      1. Shasta Indians—Folklore.   2. Tales—California.   [1. Coyote
  (Legendary characters)—Legends. 2.Shasta Indians—Folklore.
  3. Indians of North America—California—Folklore.]   I. Title.
  E99.S33.C37 2002
  398.2'089'97—dc21

2002010285

Cover and Interior Art: Mary J. Carpelan
Printing and Binding: Bang Printing, Brainerd, MN

Orders, inquiries, and correspondence should be addressed to:
        Heyday Books
        P. O. Box 9145, Berkeley, CA 94709
        (510) 549-3564, Fax (510) 549-1889
        www.heydaybooks.com

Printed in the United States of America

10 9 8 7 6 5 4 3 2 1

Author's Note

My grandfather, Fred L. Wicks, used to tell this story to my sisters and brothers and me all the time, even when we got older. We never got tired of hearing it. My great-great-aunt Clara Wicks used to tell it to my mother when she was a child, as they were going up on Quartz Hill to the *icknish* patch in the spring. Mom said that she always watched the mountains to the west to make sure there were no clouds.

Icknish is wild celery, *Lomatium californicum*. It is one of the first plants to grow in the spring. The people used to place large, flat rocks on the plant to get really long, tender shoots. When the plants get older they tend to get spicy hot. *Icknish* is also our sacred root. It is used as sage is used; it keeps bad spirits and bad people away from you. When someone doesn't like the smell of *icknish*, you know you cannot trust them.

The three days that Coyote tries to shoot the sun are the three days of the spring equinox. Quartz Hill, Duzel Rock, and Mount Shasta line up with the southern *icknish* patch. And if you look closely at the rock pile, you can still see Coyote waiting.

Mary J. Carpelan

Coyote lived in Quartz Valley with his family. He had two girls.

They stored food for the winter. They had dried fish, dried deer meat, acorns, and manzanita berries.

the food they ate was stored away in bins.
d they lived all winter on it, in a cave.

Well, springtime came. Sun came out bright in March, and Coyote looked out and thought, "Ohhhh, for sure spring is here." He hollered, "Ohhhh girls, go and get some *icknish!* Throw all the old food out. Throw it down the hill.

"We will get new food now. All the fresh food
is blooming, getting ready to ripen.
Sun is shining bright."

So the girls threw all the food out,
down the hill.

And so he said, "All right now, go get some *icknish*. *Icknish* should be ripe now up on Quartz Hill."

"There are two *icknish* patches there, one near the top and one down the south side of the hill. Big open spot on the hillside. No brush grows there, just *icknish*."

Well, they went. Up the hill they went, an big cloud came over, and it started to snow

It got two feet deep! It was one of those early springs—it comes in March, and later it snows again before real summer comes.

Coyote was fooled. He was mistaken, and his girls never came home that night. They froze to death.

And the next morning, Coyote went looking for them. He finally found them, frozen to death in the snow, so he got mad.

He didn't have anything to eat. Food all gone. So h
blamed the sun for coming out too early. Fooled hi
So he decided he would shoot the sun.

...n came up over Oro Fino Hill in the morning, so ...went over there and sat upon the hill, waiting for ...sun to come up. And the sun came up behind ...zel Rock, Moffett Creek. "Ohhhh," Coyote said, ... must have seen me waiting here for him, so he ...es up over there."

So he headed for Duzel Rock, and he got there at nighttime, in the dark. And he hid himself behind the rocks and waited for the sun to come up in the morning, so he could shoot him.

Sun comes up way over behind Gazelle Mountain, towards Mount Shasta. "Ohhhh! He must have see me again. I'll travel all day and wait for him again."

So he went and went and finally got there, one of those big lime rocks behind Gazelle, the high one.

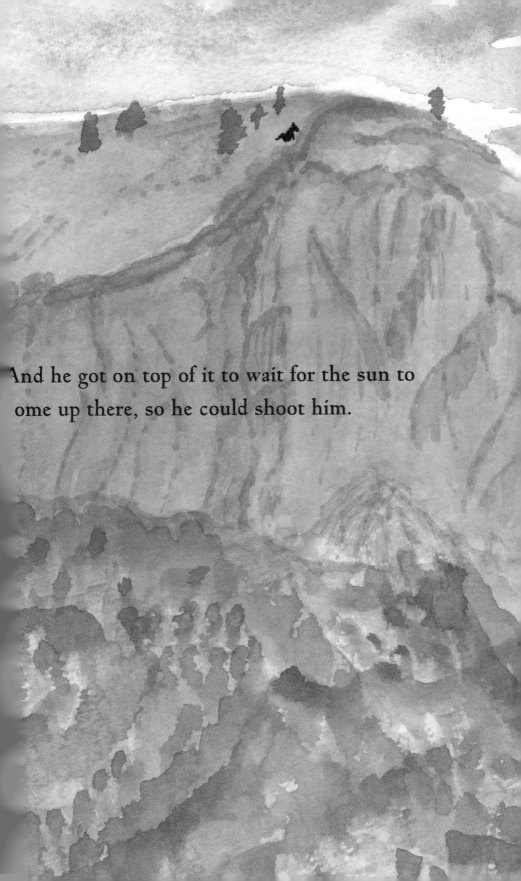

And he got on top of it to wait for the sun to come up there, so he could shoot him.

The sun came up over behind Mount Shasta the next day.

"Ohhhh! He saw me again," Coyote says. So he went down the hill, and there was a big lake there. But it was a valley of fog—he thought it was a lake.

"Ohhhh, good! I'll take a swim. I'll swim across over to Mount Shasta."

So he dove in. Down the mountain he went, end over end. Over the rocks and bluffs.

Down to the bottom of the valley he rolled. He got up and he went a little farther, and he got up on a rock pile near Gazelle.

And he is still sitting there, waiting fo
the sun to come up so he can shoot.

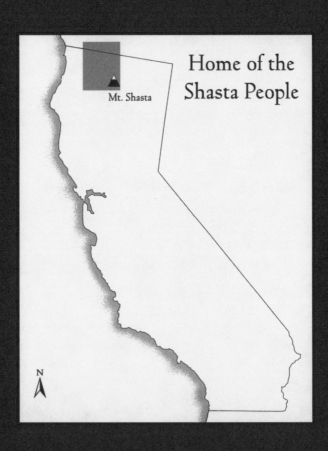

Mt. Shasta

Home of the
Shasta People

N

The Shasta

The traditional home of the Shasta people extends from north central California into southern Oregon, encompassing most of today's Siskiyou County in California and parts of Jackson and Klamath Counties in Oregon. The Shasta people hunted deer, fished for salmon, and gathered plants for food, medicine, basketry, and other purposes in a terrain distinguished by rugged elevations and extreme weather. Mount Shasta is their most distinctive landmark, and like the other tribes around the mountain (Achumawi and Wintu), they have a rich body of story and tradition not only about this mountain but about other features of the landscape, both large and small.

MARY J. CARPELAN is of Shasta and Cahuilla heritage—her maternal grandparents met at Sherman Indian School in Riverside, California. Born and raised in Siskiyou County, she grew up listening to the stories that her great-grandfather and grandfather told her. She graduated from Humboldt State University with a degree in social welfare, worked in archaeology for nineteen years, and has now embarked on a career in writing and painting.